What were castles for?

Phil Roxbee Cox

Illustrated by Sue Stitt & Annabel Spenceley

Designed by Diane Thistlethwaite & Vicki Groombridge

Series editor: Jane Chisholm
History consultant: Anne Millard
With thanks to Andy Dixon

CONTENTS

What were castles for?

Castles were places for lords and their families to live in. They were built to keep out enemies and to keep people, horses and treasures safe.

Horses were very important because armies couldn't get very far very quickly without them.

This is what some of the very early castles looked like. This type of castle is called a motte and bailey.

All the fences and walls are built of wood.

The large courtyard is called the bailey.

This mound of earth was called the motte.

This huge castle was built in the Middle East in the 13th century.

Thick stone walls

Battlements

This castle fortress was built in the Sudan, about 4000 years ago.

What did castles look like?

Very different from each other. Early stone castles had just one square tower in the middle, called a keep. Later castles were made up of many buildings.

Castles have been around for a very long time, but the great age of castle-building was in the Middle Ages. Most of the castles in this book come from then.

This Japanese castle was built in the 17th century.

What and when were the Middle Ages?

The name later given to a period of European history. Things that happened in, or come from, the Middle Ages are called "medieval".

The Middle Ages started in about the 11th century and ended in about 1500.

A century is a hundred years. The 11th century was from 1001 to 1100, and the 12th century from 1101 to 1200, and so on.

So medieval castles had about 500 years to develop and change in.

Who built them?

Kings, princes, lords and land owners had castles built. Skilled and unskilled workers actually built them. Skilled workers included stone carvers, called stone masons. Unskilled workers did all the pulling, pushing and lifting.

Where were castles built?

In areas where land needed to be protected from enemies. Once it was decided to build a castle, the best site was chosen. Castles needed a supply of water, a good view of surrounding land and as much natural protection as possible. Castles were often built on hills for defence. Some castles added a moat.

This scene shows men building a castle in Europe in the Middle Ages.

This is a simple kind of crane, made of wood.

This person is about to take the quick way down.

Mortar. A kind of cement for fixing the stones in place.

This man is in charge of the building works.

Stones arriving from the quarry

A worried worker

This man is learning to be a mason.

A wobbly wheel

Wooden scaffolding

What was a moat?

A wide, deep ditch full of water running all the way around a castle. A moat was dug to keep out unwanted visitors. People were only let in across a well-guarded bridge.

   A moat made it very difficult for an attacking army to tunnel under the castle's walls. The tunnel would fill with water.

Carpenters

3

What did they keep in a keep?

The most important people and their belongings. This was because the keep was the safest place there was. It kept out enemies and bad weather.

This is what the keep of an early medieval castle looked like. The holes in the walls haven't been made by cannon fire. They have been put there by the artist so that you can see inside.

Who actually lived in the keep?

Not just the lord and lady of the castle and their family, but their servants and knights too. These included men-at-arms, pages, squires, ladies-in-waiting and a priest.

As castles got bigger, lords and ladies had nicer rooms built in the courtyards.

Did you know?

Rich enemies weren't often held prisoner in the dungeon, but were given comfortable rooms in a castle. Their friends would then pay money for them to be let free.

The lord of the castle has lots of money. This man is counting it.

The chapel window is the only window in this keep with glass in it.

The lord and his guests are enjoying a banquet in the Great Hall.

The weapons are kept here.

The dungeon, where poor prisoners are kept.

Friends of the castle's lord

This man is keeping watch.

4

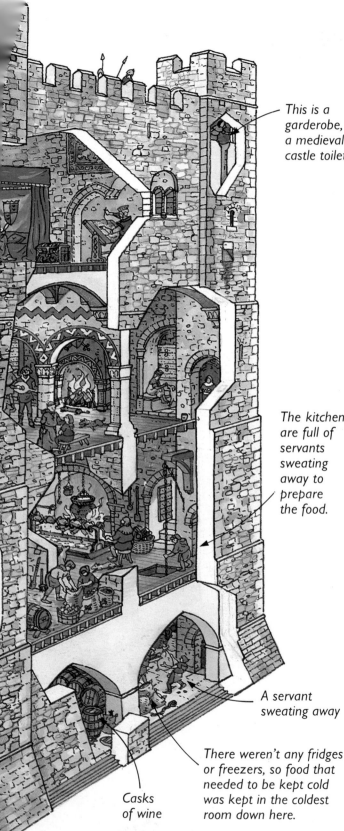

This is a garderobe, a medieval castle toilet.

The kitchens are full of servants sweating away to prepare the food.

A servant sweating away

Casks of wine

There weren't any fridges or freezers, so food that needed to be kept cold was kept in the coldest room down here.

Did they have toilets?

Sort of. There were pots in the lord and lady's bed chamber, which is how they came to be called chamber pots. Servants had to empty them.

There were also things called garderobes. These were seats above chutes set in the outer walls of the keep.

Where do you think . . . ?

Where do you think that the waste from the garderobe went? What problems might this have caused?

Where did they sleep?

The rich had cosy beds with curtains around them. The servants were less lucky. They had to bring out their thin straw mattresses and sleep wherever they could. This was often in the Great Hall.

Did they have baths?

Yes, baths were tubs like barrels. Some of these were so big that people needed steps to climb into them.

Even the noblest of nobles didn't have baths very often. The tubs were carried into the bedroom when they were wanted.

A servant carries buckets of hot water from the kitchen to the lord's bed chamber.

What went on inside the castle walls?

It depends. A castle was its lord's home. It was a place to store the money and food he took from his lands. But, in times of trouble, it was also where his people would go for protection. After a time, people stopped building keeps. Rooms were built into castle walls.

Who could live inside the walls?

As well as the nobles and servants, there were armourers, smiths, fletchers, ostlers, falconers and dog handlers.

Armourers made armour for the soldiers. Smiths made horseshoes. Fletchers made arrows. Ostlers looked after the horses. Falconers trained birds called falcons.

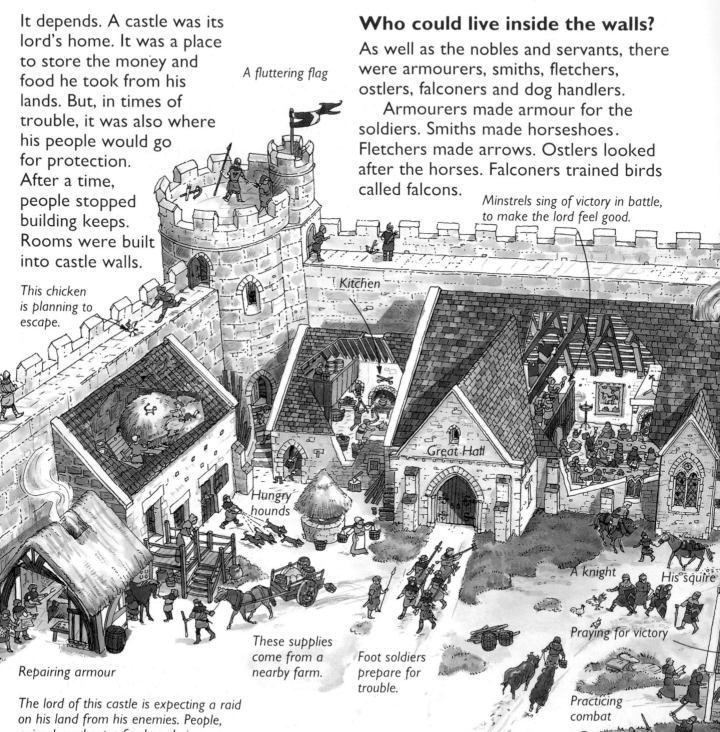

A fluttering flag

Minstrels sing of victory in battle, to make the lord feel good.

This chicken is planning to escape.

Kitchen

Hungry hounds

Great Hall

A knight

His squire

Praying for victory

Repairing armour

These supplies come from a nearby farm.

Foot soldiers prepare for trouble.

Practicing combat

The lord of this castle is expecting a raid on his land from his enemies. People, animals and extra food are being brought inside the castle walls for safety.

6

What farm animals did they keep?

Very few. Most farm animals were kept on farms. But they did keep chickens, geese and ducks inside the walls.

Some castles had lofts full of pigeons too. If a castle was under seige, bigger animals would be brought inside for protection.

What is a drawbridge?

The answer is best explained with pictures.

This castle has been built on the side of a cliff. This is so that the lord can protect his land from enemies coming from across the sea.

Lookouts looking out

Someone in a spot of bother

Castle entrance

Huge chains

Drawbridge (open)

Moat

Chain

Wheel for winding up chains

Weight

Drawbridge

Moat

This last picture shows the chains wound right up so that the drawbridge is now closed. The bridge has now become a huge closed door. This leaves no easy way to cross the moat, which helps to keep out the enemy.

7

What did nobles do for fun?

Noblemen and noblewomen enjoyed big meals, listening to songs, watching jousts (see pages 24-25) and hunting. Later, dancing became popular too.

How did nobles hunt?

They would always be on horseback. Sometimes they hunted with a pack of hounds and sometimes enjoyed a different kind of hunting called falconry.

This scene shows a medieval deer hunt. You may be pleased to know that, this time, only one will get caught. The hunt is taking place in the land belonging to the lord of the castle.

There is someone up this tree. He is hiding, which is why you can't see him.

Traps for catching rabbits

A noble. That is why he is on a horse.

What did they hunt?

Stags, bears, wolves, deer, rabbits and birds were all popular victims of a hunt.

Poor people often hunted on their lord's land too, usually for something to eat. This wasn't allowed and was called poaching. If they were caught, they were given horrible punishments.

This stag is about to make a clean getaway.

What is falconry?

Using specially trained birds, called falcons, to catch and bring back small animals.

Falconry was very popular with both lords and ladies.

Wild boar hiding from the hunters

These ladies are enjoying themselves with their falcons.

A trained falcon

This horse is stopping for a quick bite to eat.

What else did women do for fun?

Embroidery was very popular, but shouldn't be muddled with tapestry. A noblewoman would embroider small items such as cushion covers.

Tapestries were much bigger and usually made by weavers.

This noble lady is embroidering a cushion cover. It's rather good.

Tapestry of a hunting scene

How was a falcon trained?

With a lot of hard work, care and patience.

Falconer

Falcon

Thick glove

The bird learns that its food comes from its master.

The bird learns to wear a hood, covering its eyes.

Leather rein

With the hood off, but on a rein, the falcon flies after scraps of food thrown in the air.

Bird killed by falcon

Finally, the falcon flies free, attacking small birds, then returning to the falconer. Now it is ready to hunt for a nobleman or woman.

Who or what were knights?

All knights were men, but very few men were knights.

You had to be "of noble birth" and train as a page and a squire first. (See over the page.)

A knight swore to be faithful to his king and country and to his church.

A knight was addressed with "Sir" in front of his name.

To be recognized easily, he had a coat-of-arms on his shield.

What did knights wear?

In battle and tournaments, knights wore armour. The first armour was made of thick leather, and links of metal called chainmail.

Later, it was made up of very tough pieces of metal fixed together with joints.

This is called a morning star. It's about to make a dent in the other man's head, as well as his helmet.

This knight is fighting for his lord, so he has his lord's coat-of-arms on his shield.

Knights' horses were big and chunky like these two. They had to be, to carry the weight of a knight in full armour.

What is a coat-of-arms?

A design made up of special pictures and symbols.

Every rich family had one. They wore it on their clothes, armour and shields so that people could recognize them in battle. When people had their helmets on, it was difficult to tell who was who.

Some simple coats-of-arms

Did armour rust in the wet?

Yes, if it wasn't looked after properly. It was the job of a knight's squire and pages to make sure it didn't rust. Everything had to be oiled and polished.

By rolling the barrel, this page is making the sand brush against his master's chainmail. This should rub off any rust.

A sweaty page

His sweat

Chainmail

Sand

Barrel

Who were the Knights of the Round Table?

Old British legends tell of a great king named Arthur. He lived in a castle called Camelot. There, he and his knights would sit and make plans at a huge round table. Because of this, King Arthur's knights were known as the Knights of the Round Table.

Did they really exist?

Arthur probably did, and he would have had men fighting for him. They would not have dressed like the knights in this book. They came from the much earlier time of around 500.

Pictures of King Arthur, like this one, often show him in a kind of armour the real king would never have seen.

More coats-of-arms

Can I design my own coat-of-arms?

Good idea. You could make up a pretend one using some of the designs on these pages.

In some countries, there are still strict rules about what you can and cannot put on your coat-of-arms.

Who could be a knight?

Men who came from "good" (rich) families, and who had gone through the hard training of being a page then a squire.
Women couldn't become knights. Neither could men from ordinary families.

This boy is going off to his uncle's castle to be a page.

Happy sister

Sad but proud parents

These boys are listening to stories of battles lost and won.

Abacus

This page is trying to do simple sums, using something called an abacus.

Lord

Lady

Part of a page's job is to serve his lord and lady's meals at table.

Meal

A tablecloth in need of good wash

What was a page?

The first stage of getting to be a knight. Boys were usually sent away from home to become pages. They learned manners, trained with weapons and were given a basic education.

Did pages learn to read and write?

In the early days, no one bothered. All knights wanted to do was to beat each other in battle. There seemed no point in being able to read or write. Later, this changed and pages were taught both.

This is the best shot so far.

This page had better move out of the way.

This page is learning archery. He hasn't managed to hit the target yet.

This page is learning to use a lance on horseback. He's fallen off three times already.

This squire is an excellent horseman. He has to be strong to carry the weight of the armour he will wear.

Young squires helping a knight put on his armour.

What did squires have to do?

Look after their knights, from helping them to dress to caring for their weapons and horses. This was the next stage after being a successful page.

How were squires knighted?

By the lord or king. He rested a sword on the squire's shoulders and declared him to be a knight. This was called "dubbing".

Coat-of-arms

The man in the armour is a squire who is going to be made a knight.

Now that this squire has become a knight, he is given a pair of spurs in another ceremony.

The lord knights the squire with a ceremonial sword.

This person is to be knighted next.

Spurs

13

What weapons did people use?

Ordinary soldiers used anything from rocks to cannons. A rock was a very good weapon when dropped on someone's head from the safety of a castle gatehouse. Proper cannons were not common until the 15th century.

Did they have guns?

Not really. There were a few very simple types of guns tried out as early as the 1320s. They were pretty useless. They could not be fired accurately, and they could easily hurt the person firing them. So the idea didn't catch on.

Arrows fired from bows were much better at hitting their targets over long distances. So they were much more popular and common.

Who used bows and arrows?

Ordinary soldiers, not knights. There were two main types of bows: crossbows and longbows. Knights' most important weapons were swords, morning stars and lances.

This army of soldiers is firing at their enemy across the valley. Only the man on the horse is a knight.

Pike staffs

Longbow

A bang

Crossbow

A cross bowman

A boy helps on the battlefield. (He is not a page.)

Loading a crossbow

This is an early type of cannon called a bombard.

This will be fired from the bombard.

Why did they use different bows?

Good question. Why do you think some bowmen used longbows and some used crossbows? Have a think about what the reasons might be. (The answer is on page 32.)

A medieval picture of someone using a longbow.

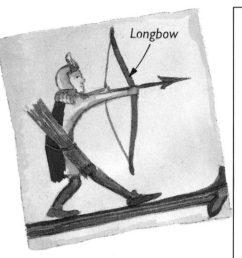

Longbow

Did they have tanks?

Although the answer is 'no', this question isn't as silly as it sounds. Medieval soldiers did use something called a siege tower. This was a huge wooden structure, full of armed soldiers, which could be wheeled right up to the side of a castle wall.

What is a morning star?

Imagine a baton with a short chain at the top attached to a metal ball covered in spikes.

The idea was for a knight to grip the baton and swing the chain around, so that the ball hit his enemy.

A morning star

A lance

This man is a sergeant at arms. He is telling the knight what has been happening.

Did you know?

We can tell what weapons and armour some noble knights used by studying their gravestones.

Some knights had pictures of themselves cut into brass and screwed onto their gravestones (which lay flat on the ground, not upright).

These pictures are called brasses.

A brass

Armour

Broadsword

Dagger

Shield

What was a castle feast like?

In good times, very filling and very noisy. What people ate depended on the period in history, the time of year and which country they were in. But wherever the feast was, whenever it was, you can be sure that there was plenty of drinking, laughing and shouting.

Where did they eat?

In the Great Hall. The most important guests and nobles sat at the "high table" with the lord and lady. Less important people sat on lower tables in front of them. Servants and peasants weren't invited to castle feasts.

A page serving

This swan has been plucked, cooked and then had all its feathers stuck back on.

This guest is unwell. Perhaps the stew didn't agree with him.

A horn full of wine

High table

People eat with their fingers and knives, but not forks.

A minstrel playing a lute

Scraps are always thrown on the floor. That is why this dog looks so pleased.

Most people are using slices of stale bread as plates. These will be handed out to the poor later.

This lower table isn't really a table, but planks resting on supports.

This boy is a young squire, training to be a knight. One of his tasks is to wait at the high table.

Bread ovens

An accident about to happen

Feeding the fire

Meat roasting on a spit

Servant roasting by the spit

Boar's head (wild pig) - a popular dish

Ducks' eggs

A hungry rat

As well as cutting apples for a pie, this boy has also cut his finger.

This picture shows part of a castle kitchen. Servants are hard at work preparing for a feast.

This cat is supposed to be catching rats.

What did nobles usually eat?

Fish on Friday and salted meat in winter. The meat was stored in salt in autumn so that it would last. They didn't have fridges or freezers to keep food fresh.

Where was it cooked?

In the kitchens, of course. In some castles, like the one on page 5, the kitchens were in the keep. In other castles, the kitchens were in sheds in the courtyard.

How was it cooked?

Vegetables were boiled and meat was usually roasted on a huge spit in front of an open fire. The fat dripping from the meat was collected and spread on pieces of bread.

What is a famine?

When there isn't enough food to eat. This happened when crops didn't grow because of bad weather. Famine could also be caused by people's enemies destroying their food supply. **17**

Where did people who didn't live in castles live?

In the countryside around the castle, or in villages. Most people were peasants. This meant they didn't own the land they lived and worked on. The land belonged to the lord of the local castle. Only a few people lived in towns.

What were peasants' homes like?

Small and basic. Often cottages had only one room. The roofs were thatched, the floors were just earth, and there was no glass in the windows. The walls were often made of wattle-and-daub.

This village has been built near a river, so that people can get their water from it.

Watermill

Church

Fed up fisherman

Pilgrims

A puddle

What is "wattle-and-daub"?

Wattle is a frame of wooden stakes with long twigs woven between them. Daub is a kind of plaster that was smeared on top of this, to make a smooth, thick wall.

Wooden stakes

Woven twigs

Daub

Vegetable garden

Local fair

18

A village wouldn't have both a windmill and a watermill. The artist has drawn both so that you can see what they look like.

A hungry wolf about to eat a thief about to attack a man on a horse.

Windy washing

Inn

Stable

What did they do for a living?

Most people worked on the land. They grew crops and raised animals. In good times, they usually had enough to eat and live off. Most of what they produced went to the lord in his castle.

What went on in a village?

This was where country people came to meet together, eat together, and pray together.

There would also be a market square for buying and selling, and travellers could sleep at a local inn.

Was it safe living in the country?

Not very. Hungry wolves in winter, and thieves on the road made the country quite a dangerous place. Villages didn't have the protection of high walls or guards.

19

 There's more on the next page.

People who didn't live in the countryside, or in castles, lived in towns. Towns often grew up around castles. Over the centuries, many of these castles have fallen into ruin or gone completely, but the towns are still there.

Who lived in towns?

Mostly craftspeople, traders, merchants, and their families. People working in the same trade often lived in the same street. Craftspeople often set up societies called guilds.

These people had easier lives than the peasants working in the country.

This scene shows what a medieval town might have looked like.

There used to be just the castle here. Over the years, the town has built up in front of it.

The guildhall, where members of the guilds meet

Market square

Church

Shops

Repairing a roof

Watermill for grinding corn

The thick walls and guarded towers are to keep enemies out.

Drawbridge

Someone is dropping things on this man.

Grain store for storing grain

There's a monastery just over the hill.

Did they keep animals?

Not farm animals. They did keep horses, for transport. Fleas, lice, mice and rats were also a common sight . . . not that people wanted them around! Dogs probably caused trouble too.

This house is on fire. It shouldn't be.

People often meet in the rooms above this gateway.

Many houses have vegetable gardens.

School house

Were towns smelly?

Indeed they were. People didn't have washing machines, bathrooms or toilets. They slopped their waste into the street.

The houses in this part of town have tiled roofs, not thatched ones. This means that the richer people live here.

This wagon is full of things to sell at market, but it's hard to tell what.

Another drawbridge

Hospital run by monks

He's just caught an old shoe, but thinks it's a fish.

Traders bring in goods by river.

What was a monastery?

A building full of monks. These were men who had chosen to serve God in a special way. A nunnery was like a monastery, except it was for women called nuns.

Monks and nuns made special promises called vows. They vowed not to own any property, not to marry and to obey the people in charge.

Who was in charge?

The Abbot or Prior or, in a nunnery, the Abbess or Prioress. Monasteries and nunneries followed strict rules. These were first made by a Christian saint called Benedict.

This picture is of a monastery. Some walls have been left out so that you can look inside.

People have come to see the bones of a saint kept here. They are given food and shelter for the night.

These monks are hard at work in the fields.

Church

The cloister - a covered walkway and courtyard.

Stained glass

Flowers

Dormitory, where the monks sleep.

Kitchen

Vegetable garden

How could you get to be a monk?

You had to be a man and be a Christian. You started off as a novice. This meant that you had to follow the rules and learn the ways of the monastery.

Only then could you take your vows and become a true monk. Some people found this too hard. Others went on to spend their whole lives serving God.

What exactly did monks do?

Apart from worshipping privately and together, they often nursed the sick, taught, gave food and money to the poor and tried to help people. Monks also grew food, made beer, and kept bees. It was a hard-working but peaceful life.

This picture from a 15th century manuscript shows a woman writing a manuscript.

Monks on the move

Guesthouse

Abbot's house

The Abbot

Visitors

The chapter house, where monks meet.

Did you know?

In the Middle Ages, very few people could actually read or write. All early written records of local events were kept by monks or nuns. These were usually beautifully decorated documents, written with a pen called a quill. They are called illuminated manuscripts.

Can I make my own manuscript?

You can try, but it will take years to be really good at it. You could make your own quill pen.

First, you need a large feather. A goose's feather would be best. To make the nib, you need to cut the end as shown. (Be careful.)

Use a different quill for each coloured ink.

Now you're ready to dip it in ink and try writing with it.

What was a joust?

A mixture between a mock battle and a fun day out. Knights would fight each other on horseback in front of cheering, and booing, crowds. The knights weren't supposed to kill each other, but sometimes they did by mistake.

What was 'trial by combat'?

This was when two knights actually meant to kill each other, as an official way to settle an argument. This shouldn't be confused with a joust.

A pickpocket

A dancing bear

A trumpeter

The lord of the castle

A crown of laurels for the winner

The herald. His job is to call out the names of the knights in each contest.

These seats have the best view of the action. The richest and most important people are in here.

This guard is watching the joust when he should be keeping an eye out for trouble.

These entertainers are hoping people will throw them some coins.

Did they have prizes?

Yes, but they weren't valuable. However, the winner would be offered the loser's armour and horse. He could either keep it, or sell it back to the loser. Some knights made a living this way, going from joust to joust.

This knight was hurt earlier on in the day. His injury isn't as bad as he thinks.

These peasants don't get seats to sit on or a canopy over them.

A short jousting lance. Some lances were much longer.

A charging knight

The charging knight's charger

Ale tent

An archery contest

Wrestlers

This monk is speaking out against the joust, because people might be hurt.

These dogs are having a fight of their own.

A marshall watching the contest

A poor beggar

Did they have a referee?

Yes. He was called a marshall. It was his job to make sure that everyone played by the rules and didn't cheat.

How were castles defended?

Very well in most cases. Castles were built for defence and were hard to attack. They had high stone walls, small windows, and battlements for soldiers to hide behind.

Some even had deep moats full of water all the way around them, and a drawbridge that could be pulled up.

This scene shows the second day of the attack on this castle. The artist has 'cut away' part of the tower so you can see inside.

Battlements

Machicolations. Rocks will be dropped through these.

This iron gate is called a portcullis It can be raised or lowered.

Battering ram for knocking down the gate. If they can cross the river, that is.

Catapult

The drawbridge is up to keep out unwanted visitors.

Sinking soldier

These large wicker shields are to protect them from things thrown or fired from the castle.

Did they really pour boiling oil on the enemy below?

Yes, but not very often. High up in the battlements were special holes, called machicolations. Usually, rocks and timber were thrown down them.

What was a siege?

When an attacking army tried to stop anyone getting in or out of the castle. When the food ran out, the people inside would either have to give up and surrender, or starve to death.

This leg has just kicked away the ladder.

The attackers at the top of the seige tower are running onto the battlements.

These extra defences were built weeks ago. The lord knew trouble was coming.

A dropped crossbow

Going down

Arrowslit windows. Thin enough to fire out of. Very difficult for the enemy to fire into.

Brave soldiers

A seige tower, full of soldiers, has been wheeled up to the wall.

Rocks for firing

A larger, slingshot, catapult

A tunnel, held up with wooden props, has been dug under the wall by the attackers. They are now burning the props. This should make the tunnel cave in and the wall fall down - they hope.

What weapons did an attacking army use?

Plenty, and many of them are shown on this page. These include catapults, siege towers and also battering rams.

What was a battering ram for?

Ramming into doors and gates to smash holes for soldiers to get through. The very first battering rams were just logs.

Later, battering rams were put on wheels and covered over to protect the soldiers pushing them from being shot with arrows.

27

What were the crusades?

They were "holy wars", fought by Christians against the Moslem Turks, starting in the 11th century. They were called "holy" wars because the fight took place in the Holy Land, between people with different religious beliefs.

Where is the Holy Land?

In what is now Israel, Jordan and Lebanon.

Before the crusades, Christians went there to visit the holy city of Jerusalem, which was ruled by the Arabs.

Why was there a war?

In the 11th century, the Arabs were conquered by a people called the Seljuk Turks. They made the visiting Christians unwelcome, and made them pay to visit Jerusalem. As a result, armies of Christian crusaders marched to Jerusalem to try to take it over.

This crusader was wounded in battle.

Spices

This scene shows a group of crusaders back in Europe. They've brought some wonderful things back with them from the Holy Land.

This beautiful carpet is a treasured possession.

This dog is pleased that his master is back home again.

This is a spice called saffron. Even today it is more expensive than gold.

Who won?

The crusades lasted over 200 years. The Christians won Jerusalem . . . then lost it. In the end, the city stayed under the rule of the Moslems.

The coloured areas on this map show Christian states set up in the Holy Land by the crusaders.

Jerusalem

HOLY LAND

Did you know?

Crusaders brought back silks, soaps and spices from the Holy Land. They also brought back the idea of having baths more often.

There are many legends about the crusades and about one man who was said to be as brave as a lion. He was the King of England. His name was Richard the Lionheart.

The Minstrel and the Lionheart

Richard the Lionheart had fought for two long, hard years in the Holy Land. His knights had won many battles thanks to his skill and bravery, but the city of Jerusalem was still in enemy hands. It was held by the Moslems, who were led by the mighty Saladin. Meanwhile, the French crusaders had gone home and King Richard had heard rumours that his brother was plotting with the French King to seize the throne of England.

Richard agreed three years' peace with Saladin, and soon set off back to England to sort out his troubles. But the journey homeward across Europe was every bit as dangerous as the crusades. . . and he disappeared.

The English court realized that their king must have been taken prisoner in Austria or Germany. But nobody knew which castle was Richard's prison. A man called Blondel, an old friend of the king, travelled to Austria to try to track him down.

Blondel was a minstrel. His job was to sing songs and tell stories. Years before, he and King Richard had even written a song together. It was this song that Blondel now sang outside every castle wall. One day, Blondel heard a voice joining in the singing from a castle tower and he knew he had found the king!

Blondel hurried back to England, where enough money was raised to pay for King Richard's freedom. Or so the legend goes. It's certainly true that Richard enjoyed music. It's also true that he was taken prisoner in Austria in 1192. But what of Blondel? Who knows? It makes a good story.

Where in the world are there castles today?

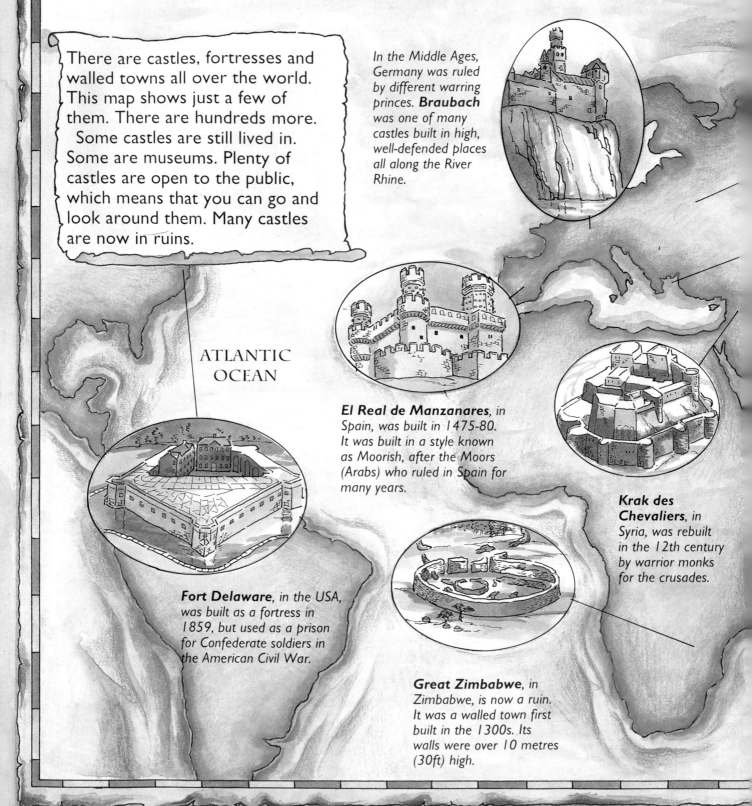

There are castles, fortresses and walled towns all over the world. This map shows just a few of them. There are hundreds more.
Some castles are still lived in. Some are museums. Plenty of castles are open to the public, which means that you can go and look around them. Many castles are now in ruins.

In the Middle Ages, Germany was ruled by different warring princes. **Braubach** was one of many castles built in high, well-defended places all along the River Rhine.

ATLANTIC OCEAN

El Real de Manzanares, in Spain, was built in 1475-80. It was built in a style known as Moorish, after the Moors (Arabs) who ruled in Spain for many years.

Krak des Chevaliers, in Syria, was rebuilt in the 12th century by warrior monks for the crusades.

Fort Delaware, in the USA, was built as a fortress in 1859, but used as a prison for Confederate soldiers in the American Civil War.

Great Zimbabwe, in Zimbabwe, is now a ruin. It was a walled town first built in the 1300s. Its walls were over 10 metres (30ft) high.

The **Kremlin** in Moscow, Russia was originally a 12th century city-fortress, built to enclose palaces, churches and other buildings.

Himeji Castle, in Japan, was built in 1609 as a defence against revolting warlords.

Amber Palace is a 16th century palace-fortress built by a local ruler in Rajasthan in India.

PACIFIC OCEAN

Crusader castles, like the castle of the **Knights of St John** in Rhodes, Greece, were built all along the route to the Holy Land.

What is a castle ruin?

A castle that has fallen down, or been pulled down so that much of it is missing. Usually it doesn't have a roof.

Some ruins are huge, and still look like castles. Others may just be a few stones. All of them can be interesting if you can find out about their history. Then you can imagine what it must have been like living there in castle times.

These people are enjoying a day out at a castle ruin.

Index

Answers

Page 5.
Dribbled down the side of the wall. Smelled terrible and could spread disease.

Page 15.
An arrow fired from a longbow travelled much further than one fired from a crossbow. But an arrow from a crossbow travels much faster.

First published in 1994 by Usborne Publishing Ltd,
Usborne House 83-85 Saffron Hill,
London ECIN 8RT, England.
Copyright © 1994 Usborne Publishing Ltd.

The name Usborne and the device are
Trade Marks of Usborne Publishing Ltd.

Printed in Belgium